For my darling son Gabriel,
king of the hypnotizing eyes . . .
I LOVE YOU — G. S.

For Mum, Dad,
Lee, Claire, and Andrew — D. T.

Atheneum Books for Young Readers
An imprint of Simon & Schuster Children's Publishing Division
1230 Avenue of the Americas
New York, New York 10020
Text copyright © 2008 by Gillian Shields
Illustrations copyright © 2008 by Dan Taylor
First published in Great Britain in 2008 by Simon & Schuster UK Ltd.
All rights reserved, including the right of reproduction in whole or in part in any form.
The text for this book is set in Rockwell.
The illustrations for this book are digitally rendered.
Manufactured in Singapore
First U.S. edition 2008
2 4 6 8 10 9 7 5 3 1
CIP data for this book is available from the Library of Congress.
ISBN-13: 978-1-4169-7127-6
ISBN-10: 1-4169-7127-0

DogFish

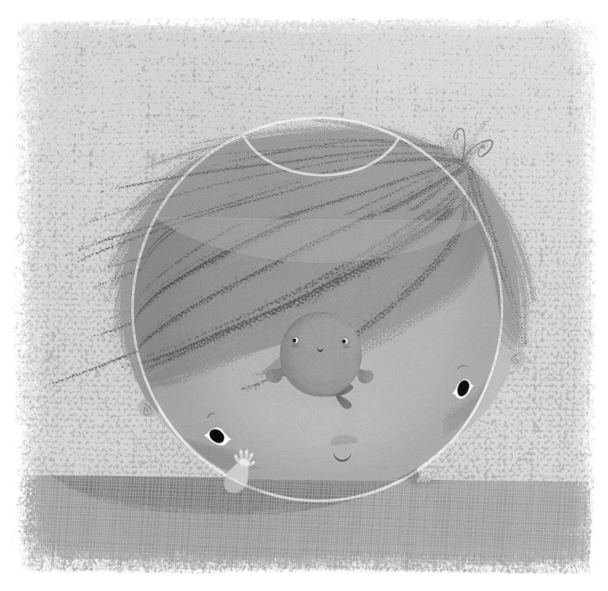

by Gillian Shields
Illustrated by Dan Taylor

ATHENEUM BOOKS FOR YOUNG READERS
New York · London · Toronto · Sydney

Everyone has a dog . . .

except me.

But my mom says,

   "Why do you need a dog when
   you have such a nice goldfish?"

She always says things like that.

catch sticks,

or go for walks,

or sit by your feet.

And they NEVER
wag their tails.

"That is why," I say, looking at her with my hypnotizing eyes,

"I NEED A DOG."

But my mom says,
"We'll see," which really means, "**NO**."

I look sad.
My goldfish looks sad too.

These are our sad looks.

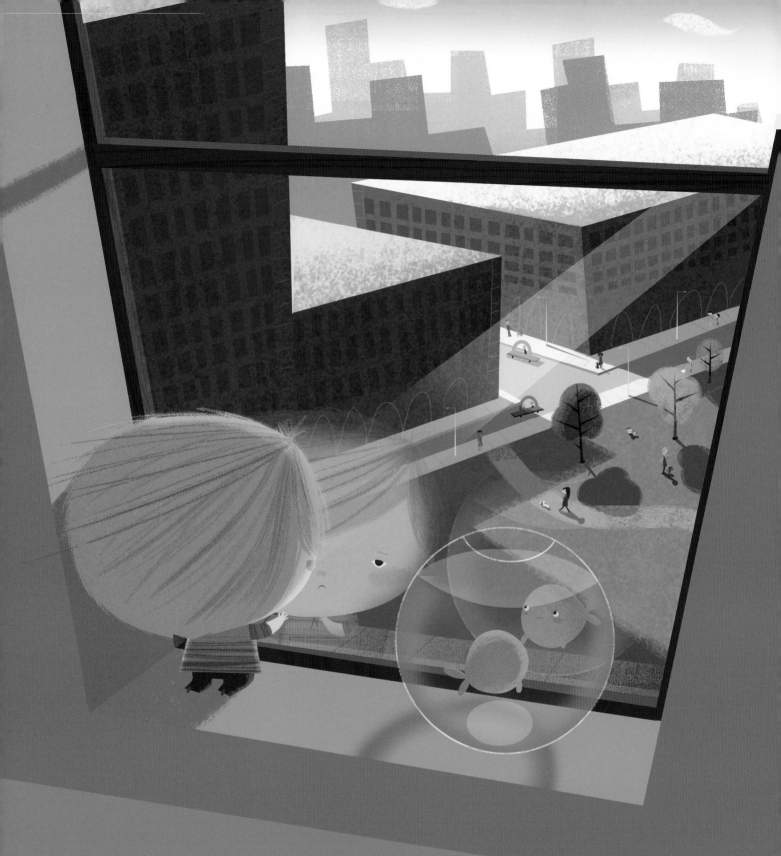

So my mom says in her kind-and-caring voice,
"But, honey, how could we have a dog
when we live on the forty-fourth floor?"

I think for a bit and then say,
"Four hundred and forty-four
stairs would be very good
exercise for a dog."

Then she says in her soothing-and-explaining voice,
"But, sweetheart, wouldn't the dog be bored
all day, when I'm at work and you're in school?"

So I think a bit more and say,
"It could read the paper."

And my mom looks irritated
but sorrowful.

Like this:

Then she says in her this-really-is-the-end-of-the-matter voice,

"Now, darling, how could we possibly afford to feed a great big hungry dog?"

But I say as quick as a fish,
"I don't want a big hungry dog. I want
a very, very, very small dog that eats
hardly anything at all. Just scraps."

Then we all look how people look when
The Situation Is Hopeless. Like this:

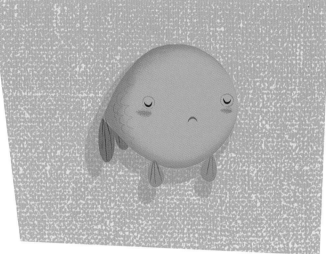

After a bit my mom says,
"Well, if you can't have what you want,
you could try to want what you have."

She ALWAYS says things like that.

So then I look at my goldfish.

And my goldfish looks at me
with his hypnotizing eyes, and I think,

Maybe . . . just maybe . . .

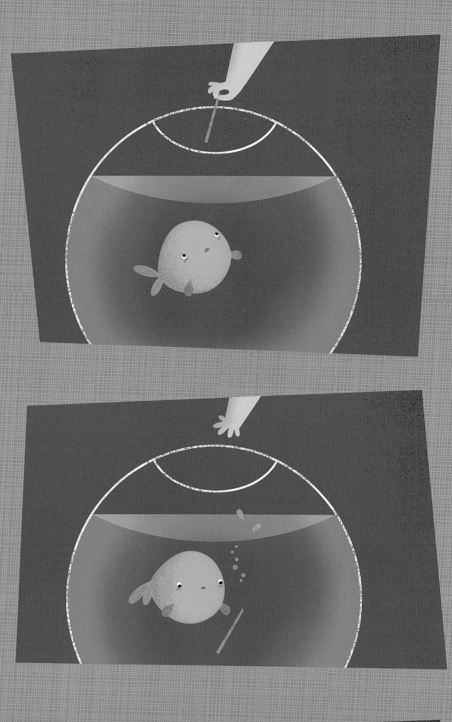

So I teach my goldfish
to catch a teeny,
tiny stick.

It takes practice.

It is a tough job.

Sometimes I think it is
a waste of
time.

But we get there in the end—and it feels good!

This is how good it feels.

I take my goldfish for walks . . .

. . . and he takes me for walks.

We climb
the four hundred
and forty-four stairs—

together.

When we are out, he reads the paper.
He's never bored.

He

eats

hardly

anything

. at all.

Just scraps.

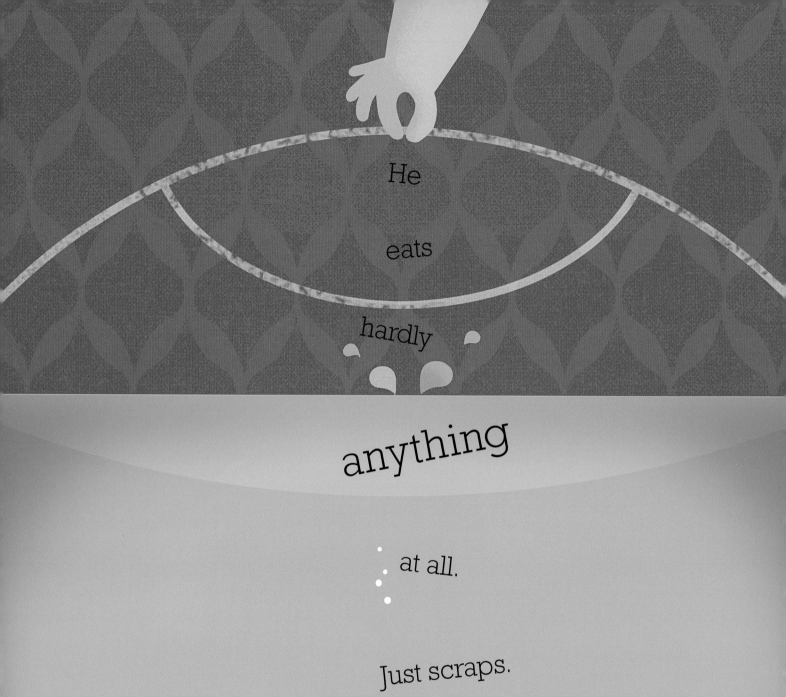

In the evening he sits by my feet,
and I tell him stuff. He's a great listener.

He can even wag his tail to say "I love you."
He's not just a goldfish . . .

He's a DOGfish!

So now when I see everyone with
their ordinary kinds of dog, I say,

"Why would I need a dog when I
have the best goldfish in the world?"

I like saying that.

And I look and my mom looks and my
goldfish looks utterly, totally, blissfully…

HAPPY!

Just like this: